Liar, Liar, Pants on Fire!

STORY BY
MIRIAM COHEN

ILLUSTRATED BY
LILLIAN HOBAN

A YOUNG
YEARLING
BOOK

Published by
Dell Publishing
a division of
Bantam Doubleday Dell Publishing Group, Inc.
666 Fifth Avenue
New York, New York 10103

Text copyright © 1985 by Miriam Cohen
Illustrations copyright © 1985 by Lillian Hoban

The trademark Yearling® is registered in the U.S. Patent and
Trademark Office.

The trademark Dell® is registered in the U.S. Patent and Trademark
Office.

ISBN: 0-440-44755-0

Reprinted by arrangement with Greenwillow Books, a division of
William Morrow & Company, Inc.

Printed in the United States of America

October 1987

10 9

WES

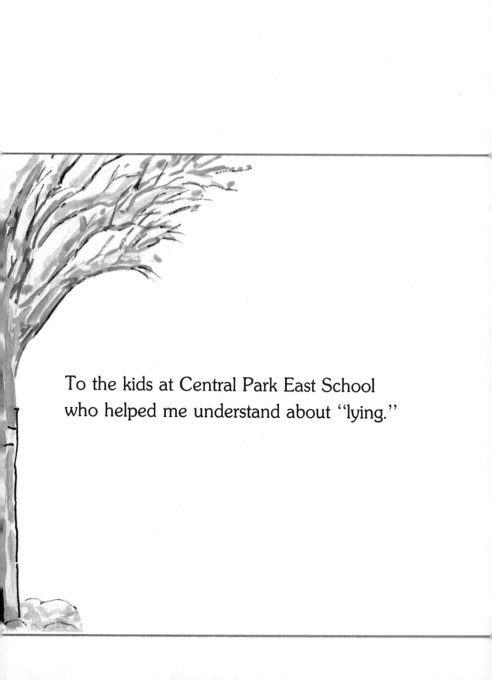

To the kids at Central Park East School
who helped me understand about "lying."

Danny told Jim what he wanted for Christmas.
"It's a racer car, with rocket shooters in the back.
And it goes one thousand miles an hour!"
"How can it go that fast?" Jim asked.
"Boosters," Danny said.

The new boy, Alex, heard them. "I've already got one of those. But mine is a triple-rocket model and it goes two thousand miles an hour."

"Has it got trick-action?" Danny wanted to know.

"Of course," Alex said.

"Let's build a fort, Jim," Danny said.

At lunch, Sara was telling about her new hamster.
"I'm going to call her Chanukah,
  because that's when I got her."

"I have a pony," Alex said.

"Is it a real pony?" George wanted to know.

"Could I see it?"

"Sometime, but not today. He's sick," said Alex.

"He hasn't got any pony," said Danny.
"How do you know?" asked Jim.

Sara said, "Alex couldn't have a pony.
He lives in an apartment."
"Alex is a liar," said Anna Maria.
"Don't play with him."

Alex went to put his lunch bag in the trash.
Paul said, "I don't like Alex. He keeps saying
he has something better than everybody else."

And when Alex came back, Danny yelled,
"Liar, liar, pants on fire!"
Everyone but Jim shouted it too.

So the teacher talked to them. She said, "Maybe Alex isn't really lying. Maybe he's just trying to get you to notice him. Try to be friends with Alex. Remember, it isn't easy to be new."

First grade was so busy getting ready
for their Christmas party, they didn't
have time to be Alex's friend.
Most of them didn't want to anyway.

First grade was going to have a tree
that they decorated themselves.

Their teacher told them they were supposed to
use only things that would be thrown away such
as plastic bottles, egg cartons, cotton,
and paper towel tubes.

Jim worked very hard on a bleach-bottle
Santa Claus. His mother gave him a red
sock for a cap because the other sock
had been lost in the laundry.

He used cotton for a beard.
And he drew the nicest, kindest face.
When he put the crayon down, he couldn't
believe he had made such a good Santa.

The morning of the Christmas party, everybody
hurried to school, carrying their decorations.

Louie's was a folded paper bird with wings that could move. Margaret had a picture of her baby brother pasted in a little cardboard box-bed. It had a tiny cotton blanket.

Willy and Sammy made a train with Santa
riding in one of the cars. "He's taking
the uptown express to our houses," they said.

Jim's Santa's cap was lost.

When he went to look for it, Alex had found it.

"Here," he said. "It was outside."

"Oh boy, thanks!" said Jim.

Everybody was laughing and running around.
The teacher said, "Line up, please! We'll take
turns putting our decorations on the tree.
Alex, didn't you make anything?"

Alex looked at the floor.
"I don't know how," he said.
   Suddenly Jim felt sorry for Alex.

He got out of line and put his bleach-bottle Santa in Alex's hand.

"Here, you can put it on the tree," he said.

Anna Maria said very loudly, "You're just
wasting your nice Santa Claus on that boy."
But the teacher smiled at Jim.

At the Christmas party, Alex was the fastest
relay runner. He won for Anna Maria's team.

George said, "Alex can run faster
than any pony!"

After the party, Alex said to Jim, "I don't really have a pony."

"That's all right," said Jim, "you're the best runner in first grade!"

Anna Maria was listening. "And that's the truth!" she said.